Out and About with
Mitchell & Dad

Hallie Durand

illustrated by Tony Fucile

CANDLEWICK PRESS

Contents

BOOK 1

Mitchell Goes Driving

1

BOOK 2

Mitchell Goes Bowling

37

For Michael Alan Steiner,
the original Remote-Control Dad
H. D.

For Eli and Elinor
T. F.

■ ■ ■

Mitchell Goes Driving

Mitchell never ever EVER wanted to
go to bed.

Until his dad finally said he could
drive there.

Mitchell was three years,
nine months, and five days
old when he got his license.

REMOTE-CONTROL DAD
DRIVER'S LICENSE

12876 77780 857873

MITCHELL
BOX 9085
SILVER MOUNTAIN ROAD

SEX HGT EYES
M 3-02 BRN

MiTChELL

First, he inspected his new car's tires.

"Good," said Mitchell.

Then he checked the engine.

"Good," said Mitchell.

And he hopped into the driver's seat.

The windshield looked a
little dirty.

So Mitchell wiped it off.

"Shiny!" said
Mitchell.

His car was an automatic, so Mitchell put it right into drive.

His car could go fast!

VROOM!

Ruh-roh.

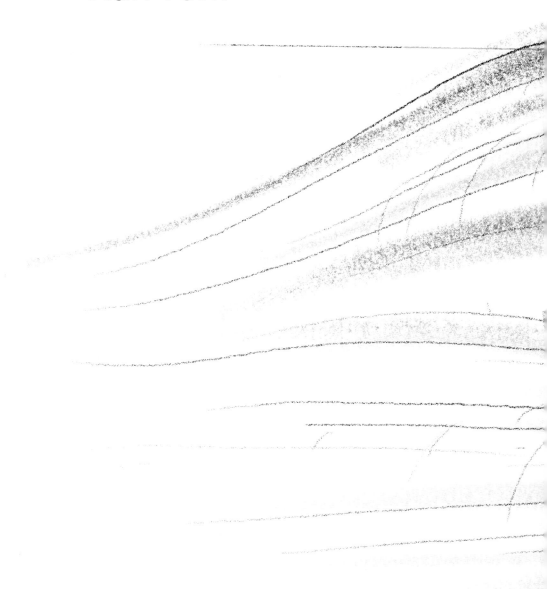

Mitchell put his car into reverse,

shifted into neutral,
and coasted to bed.

The next night, Mitchell remembered to stop and look both ways.

He also learned how to beep the horn. He liked the way it sounded . . . a lot!

Mitchell could make a left
or a right.

No blinkers needed.

And now Mitchell knew just when to press the brakes so there weren't any more collisions.

Mitchell felt comfortable behind the wheel.

In fact, he loved driving to bed!

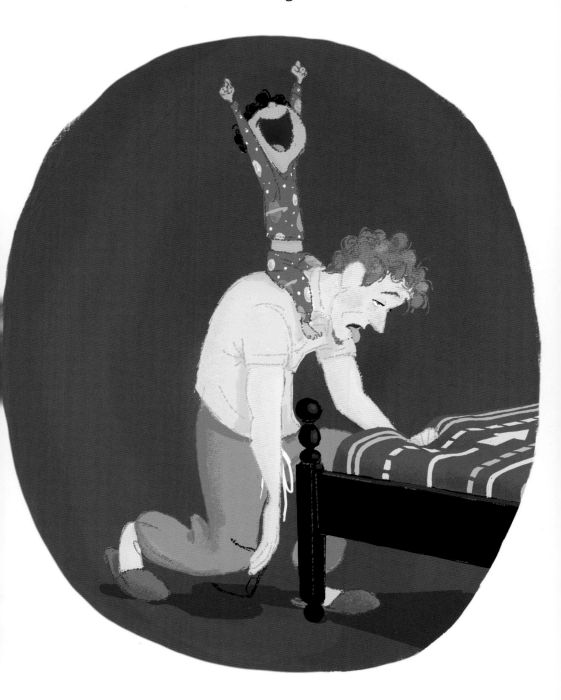

The next night, even before his bedtime,
Mitchell went to get his car.

"You need some oil," he said.

And he poured in
some oil.

The car was sputtering a
little, but Mitchell didn't
mind.

PAT
PAT
PAT

"You're OK," he said as he closed the hood.

Then he hopped into the driver's seat and backed the car out of the garage.

He slowed down for the speed
bumps in the driveway,

but when he merged onto the open road,
he really got going.

Mitchell was a great driver now, handling the hairpin turns and staying in his lane, even in two-way traffic.

They had driven a long way when Mitchell
noticed that the gas tank was on Empty.

"You need gas," said Mitchell.

Mitchell and his car took three right turns,
then a left, and beeped the horn six times.

BEEP! BEEP!
BEEP! BEEP!
BEEP!
BEEP!

Mitchell turned on his headlights and pulled up to the cookie jar.

"This is the gas station," he said.

"No," said the car.

Mitchell was surprised. The car had never spoken before.
"We need gas," said Mitchell. "Gas is a cookie."

"No gas," said the car.
"YES GAS!" said Mitchell, and he turned on his hazards. This was an emergency.

And that's when
Mitchell's car did a
U-turn

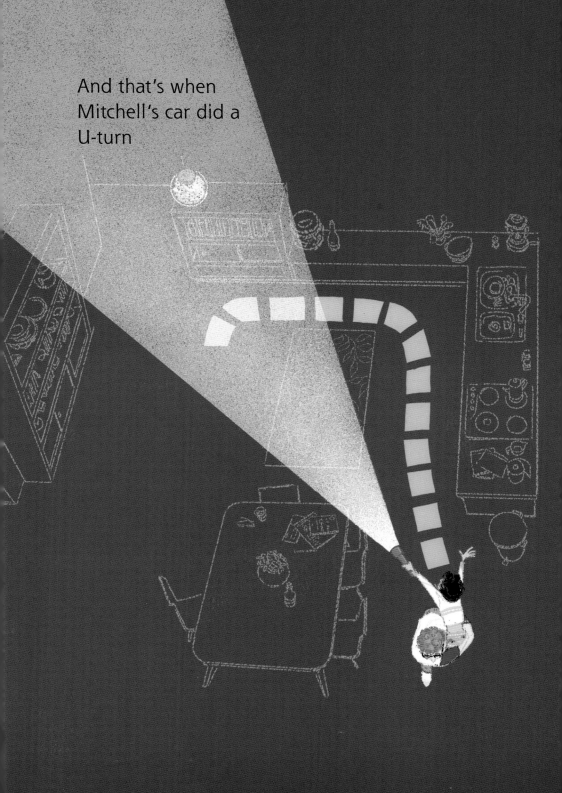

and took a shortcut, straight to Mitchell's bed.

"Will we drive again tomorrow?" said Mitchell. "As long as you stay on the road," said Dad.

And then Mitchell's dad
tucked his driver in . . .

and Mitchell drove off to find that
gas station in his dreams.

For Tony Fucile, XXX
H. D.

To Eli and Elinor
T. F.

• • •

*Big thanks to my friends Antonio and Larry at Hanover Lanes
in East Hanover, NJ.*
H. D.

Mitchell
Goes Bowling

Mitchell always knocked things down.

That's just how he rolled.

He even tried to knock down his dad. . . .

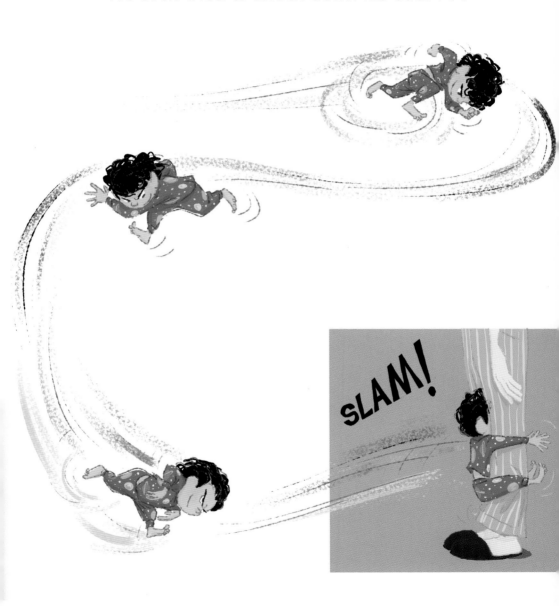

But one Saturday, when Mitchell was doing his thing, his dad caught him and put him in the car.

Mitchell didn't know where they were going,
but when they got there, he felt right at home.

There were lots of brightly colored balls,

a good pizza smell, and giant crashing noises.

Mitchell got special shoes, too.

"Lane four," the man said.
"That's how old I am!" said Mitchell.

Then he got to
type in his name.

Mitchell picked the biggest ball.

He threw it.

"That's called the gutter," his dad said.
Mitchell didn't like the gutter.

He was curious about where his ball had gone . . .

until it popped right out at him!

"You get to go again," said his dad.

Mitchell rolled and knocked two down.

"Battle on!" said Mitchell. He just knew he was going to win.

Then it was his father's turn. He backed all the way up,

swooshed toward the line,

and did a little kick with his leg.

"STRIKE!" said his dad. All the pins had gone
down, and his dad got an X.

"Oh," said Mitchell.

On Mitchell's second turn, he did
the leg kick, too. But the ball only
went a little, so Mitchell ran after it.

The lane was slippery.

That's when the people next door asked for a new lane.

53

On his next turn, Mitchell tried kicking his other leg.

"Three," said his dad. "Nice."

Mitchell's dad got another X and did a steamin'-hot-potato dance.

It was his turn again, and Mitchell got a whole side down.
He did a *double* steamin'-hot-potato dance. Then he knocked another pin down.

But he was pretty sure he was still losing.

Mitchell's dad put his hands over the blowing machine. He rolled and got another X.

So on Mitchell's turn,

he dried his hands,   his face,   and his hair,

then stuck his fingers in the holes and
did the leg kick.

He only knocked three down.

"FINE," said Mitchell. He really, really wanted an X.

He didn't get any on the next few frames.

Mitchell really wanted to win, so when he picked up his next ball, he yelled . . .

"AWAHHHHHHHHHHHHHHHHHHH!"

He THREW. . . .

He prayed. . . .

NOTHING.

"I'M GOING HOME," Mitchell said.

And that's when Mitchell's dad said, "Hey, want to be on the same team?"

Mitchell thought for a second.

With his dad, he couldn't lose.

He wanted an X. He wanted to win.

"Deal," said Mitchell.

Mitchell and his dad dried their hands,

picked up the ball,

swung their arms all the way back,

and they did a little kick.

Shhheeeeeeeeeeeeeeeeeeeeeeee—PLUNK!

That ball went sailing right down the middle and . . .

SSSSSSSSSSSSSSSSSTTTTTTTTRRR

CRRRRRRIIIIIIIIIIIKKKKKKKKKKKKE!

They did a triple steamin'-hot-potato dance, *with salsa*!

Then Mitchell looked his dad right in the eyeballs and said,

"Battle on!"

And that's just what they did.

■ ■ ■
● ● ●

The stories in this collection were previously published individually by Candlewick Press.

Mitchell Goes Driving text copyright © 2011 by Hallie Durand
Mitchell Goes Driving illustrations copyright © 2011 by Tony Fucile
Originally published in hardcover as *Mitchell's License*
Mitchell Goes Bowling text copyright © 2013 by Hallie Durand
Mitchell Goes Bowling illustrations copyright © 2013 by Tony Fucile

First edition in this format 2020

Mitchell Goes Driving
Library of Congress Catalog Card Number 2010039181
ISBN 978-0-7636-4496-3 (hardcover)
ISBN 978-0-7636-6737-5 (paperback)

Mitchell Goes Bowling
Library of Congress Catalog Card Number 2012947730
ISBN 978-0-7636-6049-9 (hardcover)

ISBN 978-1-5362-1304-1 (hardcover collection)
ISBN 978-1-5362-1167-2 (paperback collection)

20 21 22 23 24 25 TLF 10 9 8 7 6 5 4 3 2 1

Printed in Dongguan, Guangdong, China

This book was typeset in Shannon.
The illustrations were created digitally.

Candlewick Press
99 Dover Street
Somerville, Massachusetts 02144

visit us at www.candlewick.com